Clown

Guido Van Genechten

If I were a Clown,
I'd ride the wildest horses

I'd swim in the stormiest of oceans,

and march through
the roaring rains.

I'd walk on
the tightest
of tightropes,

and
meet
the
scariest
ghosts.

then I'd wish the

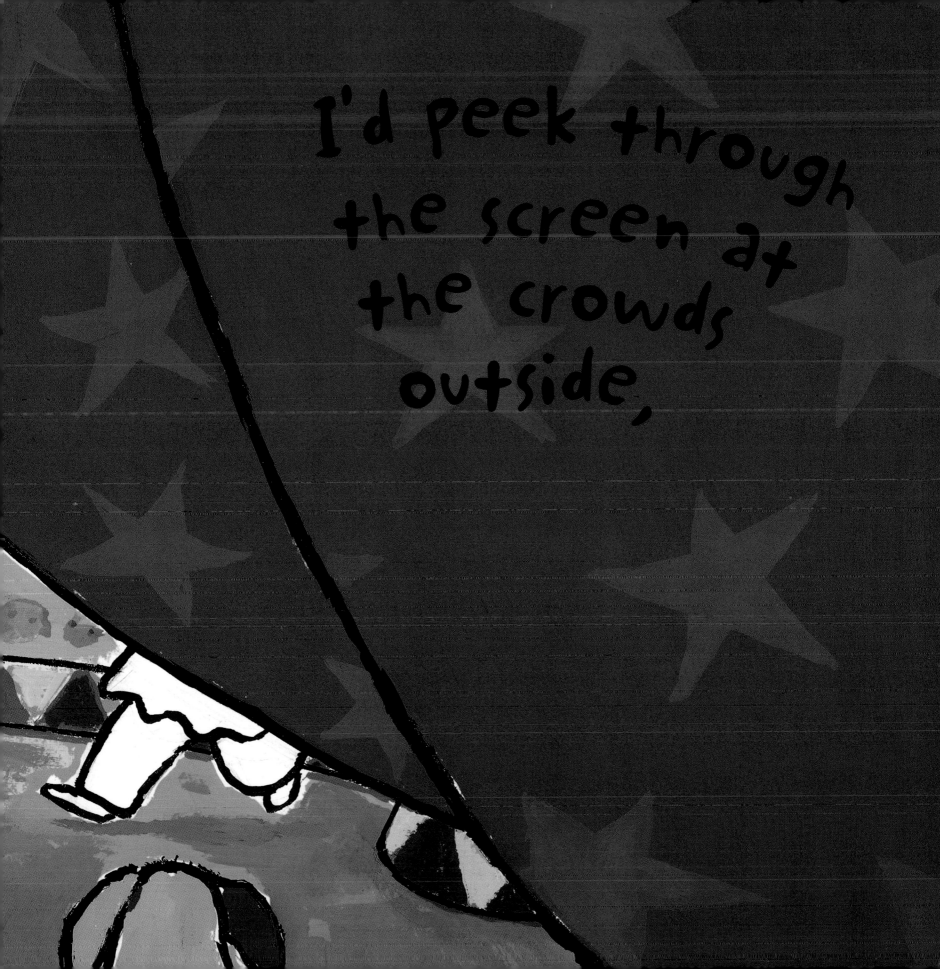

then march
out to make
them all
laugh!

Meadowside Children's Books
185 Fleet Street London EC4A 2HS

This edition published 2007

Illustrations © Guido Van Genechten 2000

The right of Guido Van Genechten to be
identified as the illustrator of this work has
been asserted by him in accordance with the
Copyright, Designs and Patents Act, 1988

A CIP catalogue record for this book is available
is available from the British Library
10 9 8 7 6 5 4 3 2
Printed in China

If I were a Clown...
I'd have the best
clown dreams
ever!